In the forest there's magic, the wonderful kind.

The kind YOU can find with the right frame of mind.

The Centipede With Too Few Feet

By Andrew Swanson
Illustrated by Bob Carnegie

For Daisy, Joshua and Samuel.

In a fabulous forest, by a shimmering stream,
Where the sunrise and sunset make waterfalls gleam,

Past the branches and bushes, trunks and tree bends,
Lay the start of a story of two special friends.

Horace lived in the forest with his sisters and brothers,

But for all of his life he'd not felt like the others.

For, in spite of his family, the hugs and mum's kissing,

Horace couldn't help feeling that something was missing.

Though his friends never said things and were all pretty cool,
Horace always felt different at Centipede School.
In his eyes all his classmates were full-grown and great,
They had one hundred feet, Horace had ninety-eight!

And the not so nice classmates (there's at least always three),
Pointed down at his legs and scoffed "How can that be?
"You've got two fewer feet than your mum and your dad,
"Having two fewer feet sure must make you feel bad."

One day all their jokes just got too much to take,

Horace started to feel the worst kind of heartache.

So he slunked out of school, through the trees, ran away,

Hoping not to feel different, at least for one day.

As the morning sun glistened and the forest lay misted,

Horace bleakly believed that no real friends existed,

But in the forest there's magic, the wonderful kind,

The kind YOU can find, with the right frame of mind.

So he shuffled along through the leaves and the rustle,

And he noticed a creature with all kinds of muscle.

A rat doing press-ups against a tree stump,

And lifting up branches, and dropping them, bump!

"Hello", said the rat, "my name is Ronnie!

"Younger brother to Richard and Robert and Johnny.

"You seem quite upset. Can I please make a mends?

"I was thinking that maybe we could become friends."

Horace sighed, "I'm not much of a creature to meet,
"I'm a poor centipede missing two of my feet.

"Everyone that I know has a hundred you see.

"Everyone else, except poor old me."

"No they don't", exclaimed Ronnie, "lookey here at the floor.

"Creatures like me only have just the four.

"Come follow me now and I'll show you, you'll see,

"Your ninety-eight feet are amazing to me."

So the pair scuttled off through a clearing ahead

And found a small mouse who was making her bed.

Ronnie pointed at Horace saying, "Look at his feet!

"He's the most awesome creature you're likely to meet."

"Well how many feet does he have?", the mouse said.

"Come, let me examine them. Sit on my bed.

"One, two...thirty-three, thirty-four!

"He's got blooming loads! I can't count anymore."

But Horace was still not convinced by their talk.

So Ronnie and he carried on with their walk.

They came to a clearing, Ronnie shouted out "Deb!"

Then a beautiful spider crawled down from her web.

"Hello old friend", Ronnie said with a hug.

"Deb, this is Horace. He's a real super bug."

Horace scoffed "He's mistaken, don't follow his lead.

"I've got two fewer feet than a real centipede."

"Well my dear boy", Deb replied with a snigger,

"People round here think that I'm special; go figure.

"And it's simply because I've got eight legs on me."

Ronnie said "That's much more than the others you see.

"But that's nothing compared to your ninety-eight.

"That really is special, you really are great.

"Ollie owl up above us has only got two.

"The cow in that field has got four, she's called Moo.

"My friend Betty Beetle has got about six.

"See, we're all very different. There's quite a good mix.

"Phil fish in that river has no legs at all.

"Willy Wasp, flying round us, has six but they're small."

"You see life would be boring if we were all just the same,

"Like if all of your class-mates had the same name.

"We've all got something that makes us unique.

"If you just look around you will see. Take a peak."

So Horace turned back a much happier creature,

Now feeling quite proud of his most famous feature.

He said, "Thank you Ronnie, for all you have done.

"I'm going home now and I'd like you to come."

"I don't know about that", frowned a worrying Ron.
"I'm not much of a rat see, you've got me all wrong.

"I'm much smaller and weaker than all of my brothers
"And I lose in arm wrestles to both my grandmothers."

"Nonsense", chirped Horace and took him inside.

And announced "This is Ronnie", beaming with pride.

Well, the school full of centipedes all gasped in awe.

"That's the most awesome creature we've seen here before!

"Horace, please tell us how you made friends with this guy?

"Our pals are all centipedes! Please tell us why?"

"It's because", Horace said "This rat's helped me see.

"That amazing things happen when I'm just being me.

"So be kind to each other, be patient and wait,

"For what's different today, tomorrow is great.

"Ronnie's my friend because he's very wise,

"He's taught me we're all special in somebody's eyes.

"And we'll say it for years when we chat and we meet,

"We might not have been friends if I had one hundred feet."

The End

If you enjoyed this book why not try
The Glower of the Glen

Written by Andrew Swanson &
Illustrated by Bob Carnegie